8 Ways to Make the Most of Storytime

FROM THE EDITORS OF

Parents.

① BE AS DRAMATIC AS POSSIBLE.

It'll help the story stick in your child's memory. You could give the mouse a British accent, make the lion roar, or speak very slowly when you're reading the snail's dialogue. Have fun making sound effects for words like boom, moo, or achoo. Encourage your child to act out movements, slithering like a snake or leaping like a frog.

② INVITE SPECIAL GUESTS.

Ask your kids if their favorite stuffed animal, action figure, or doll would like to listen too. Or curl up with the family pet. Including the whole gang will help hold their interest and make storytime seem more special. But if your child does start to lose interest before you've reached the last page, that's okay because half a book here or a quarter of a book there still counts as reading!

③ KEEP LOVINGLY WORN BOOKS IN THE ROTATION.

There's a reason your kids ask for the same title again and again: A familiar story can be as comforting as a favorite blankie. The characters become their friends, and the books serve an important emotional purpose.

④ PLAY A GUESSING GAME.

When reading a new book, pause a few times to challenge your kids to predict what's going to happen next. Encourage them to refer to the title and illustrations for clues.

⑤ REFLECT ON THE STORY.

Talk about a book for a few minutes before you move on to another. Start a conversation with statements like "I'm wondering...," "I wish I could ask the author...," and "I'm getting the idea..." This helps develop your children's intuition and their ability to communicate a story back to you.

READ TOGETHER, BE TOGETHER is a nationwide movement developed by Penguin Random House in partnership with *Parents* magazine that celebrates the importance, and power, of the shared reading experience between an adult and a child. Reading aloud regularly to babies and young children is one of the most effective ways to foster early literacy and is a key factor responsible for building language and social skills. READ TOGETHER, BE TOGETHER offers parents the tips and tools to make family reading a regular and cherished activity.

⑥ CONNECT STORIES WITH WHAT'S HAPPENING IN REAL LIFE.

Suppose you read your child a story about a baby bird, and a day or two later, you spot a tiny sparrow in the park. Ask your child, "Doesn't that bird look like the one in the book we read yesterday? I wonder if it's looking for its mommy too?" Doing so will help promote information recall and build vocabulary.

⑦ CREATE AN IMPROVISED READING NOOK.

Storytime on the sofa or a cozy chair is sweet, but wouldn't your kids lose their mind if you set up a fort every now and then? It doesn't have to be fancy: Just drape a blanket over two chairs, grab a couple of pillows, and squeeze in.

⑧ ALWAYS BE THE STORYTELLER AT BEDTIME.

You'll feel so proud when your little ones start recognizing and sounding out words on their own. But resist asking them to read to you at bedtime because it would replace this warm, wonderful bonding ritual with something that can feel like work for kids. Plus, they'll be able to listen to a more complicated book than they can read on their own.

Richard Scarry's
CARS AND TRUCKS AND THINGS THAT GO

 A GOLDEN BOOK • NEW YORK

Visit us on the Web!
rhcbooks.com

Educators and librarians, for a variety of teaching tools, visit us at RHTeachersLibrarians.com

Library of Congress Cataloging-in-Publication Data is available upon request.
ISBN 978-0-307-15785-0 (trade) — ISBN 978-0-593-30342-9 (Read Together, Be Together)

MANUFACTURED IN CHINA
10 9 8 7 6 5 4 3 2 1
2020 Read Together, Be Together Edition

fuel oil truck

garbage truck

garbage pails

auto-plane

FUEL

Have a nice trip!

garage

MISTRESS MOUSE REPAIRS

tow truck

mail van

Ma and Pa and Pickles and Penny Pig are going on a picnic. Here comes Ma with the picnic basket. Please hurry up, Ma.

MAIL

mailbox

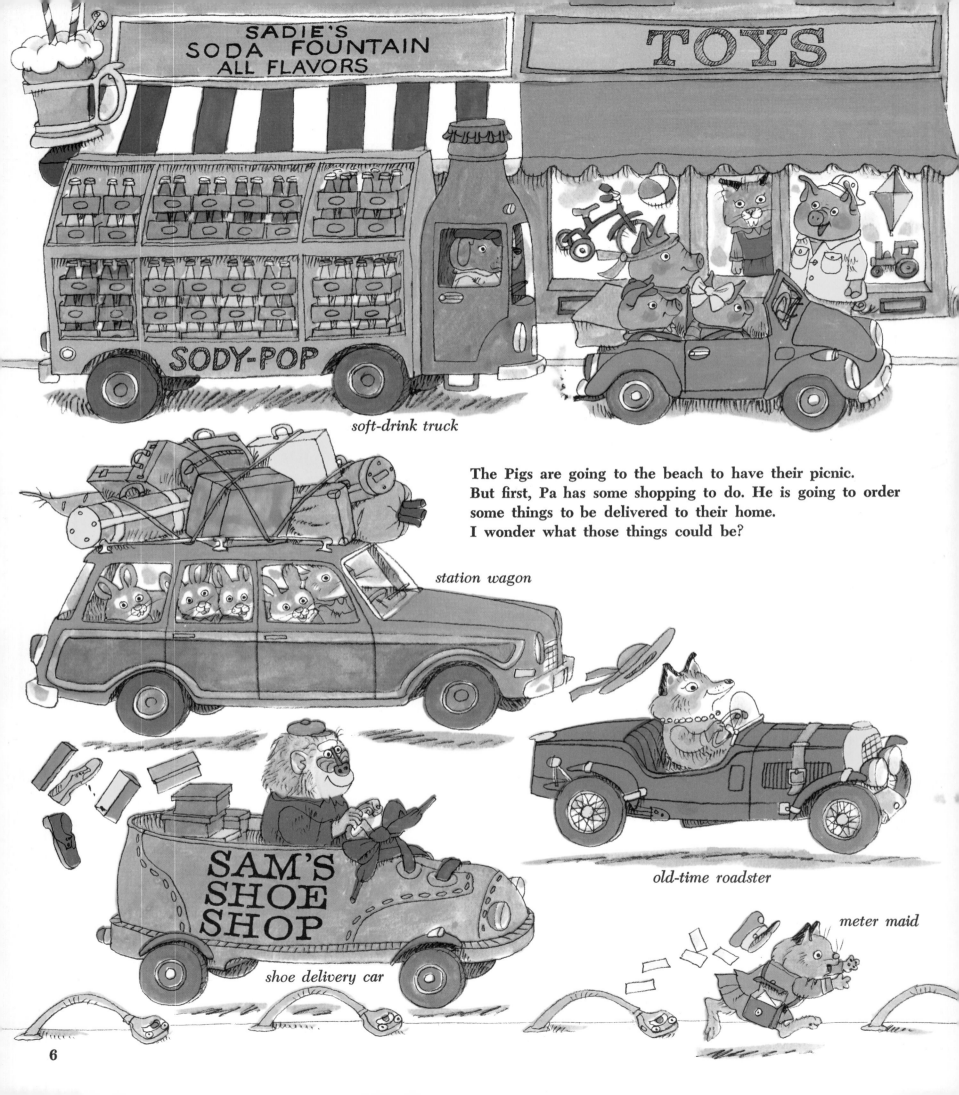

SADIE'S
SODA FOUNTAIN
ALL FLAVORS

TOYS

SODY-POP

soft-drink truck

station wagon

The Pigs are going to the beach to have their picnic.
But first, Pa has some shopping to do. He is going to order
some things to be delivered to their home.
I wonder what those things could be?

old-time roadster

SAM'S
SHOE
SHOP

shoe delivery car

meter maid

6

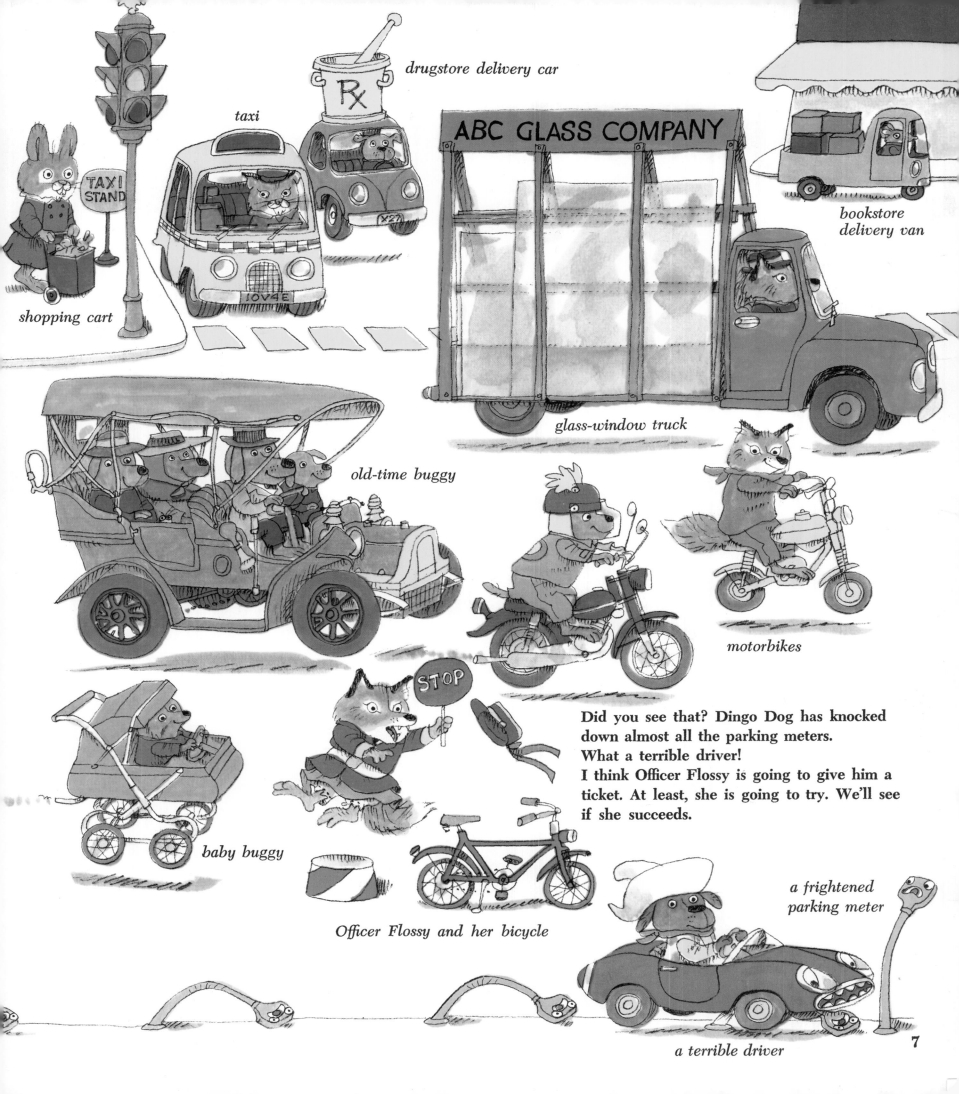

drugstore delivery car

taxi

ABC GLASS COMPANY

bookstore delivery van

shopping cart

glass-window truck

old-time buggy

motorbikes

STOP

Did you see that? Dingo Dog has knocked down almost all the parking meters.
What a terrible driver!
I think Officer Flossy is going to give him a ticket. At least, she is going to try. We'll see if she succeeds.

baby buggy

a frightened parking meter

Officer Flossy and her bicycle

a terrible driver

7

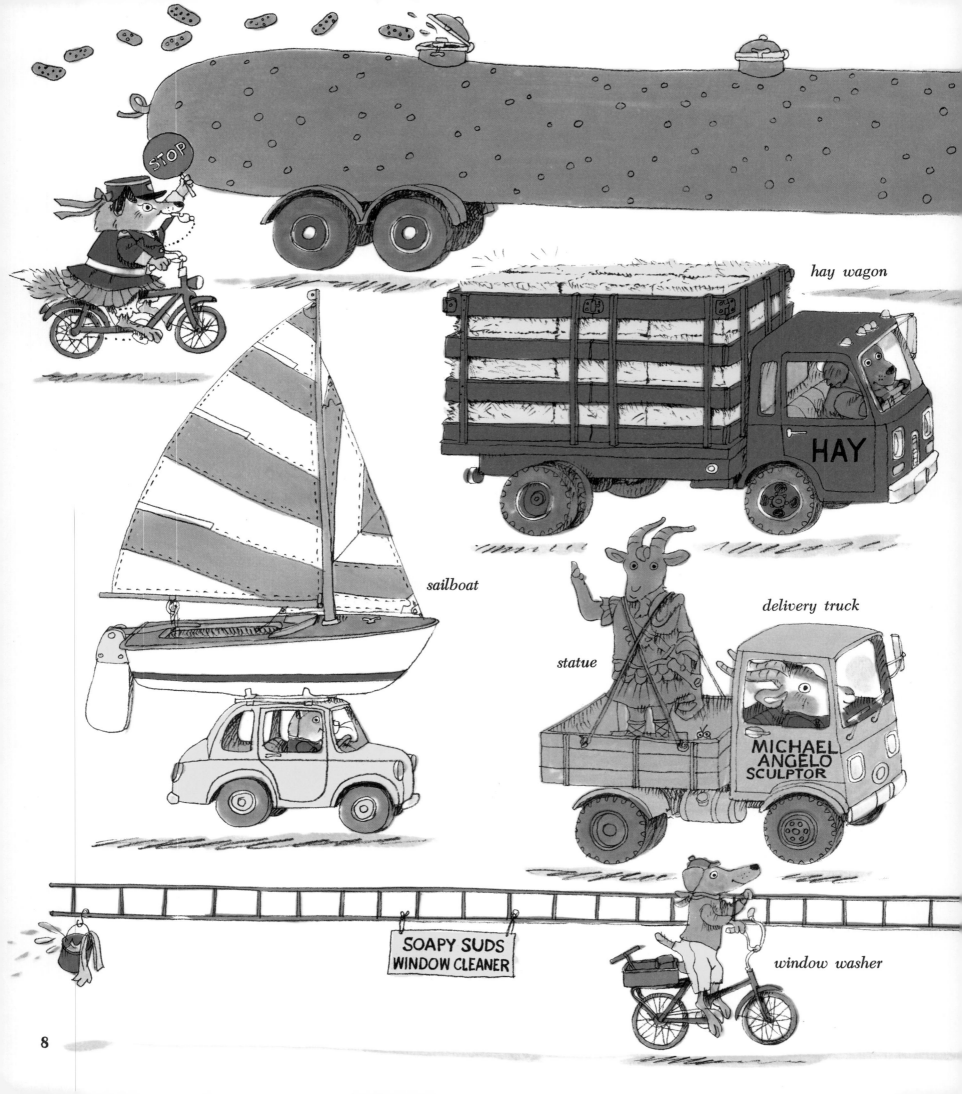

hay wagon

sailboat

statue

delivery truck

MICHAEL ANGELO SCULPTOR

HAY

STOP

SOAPY SUDS WINDOW CLEANER

window washer

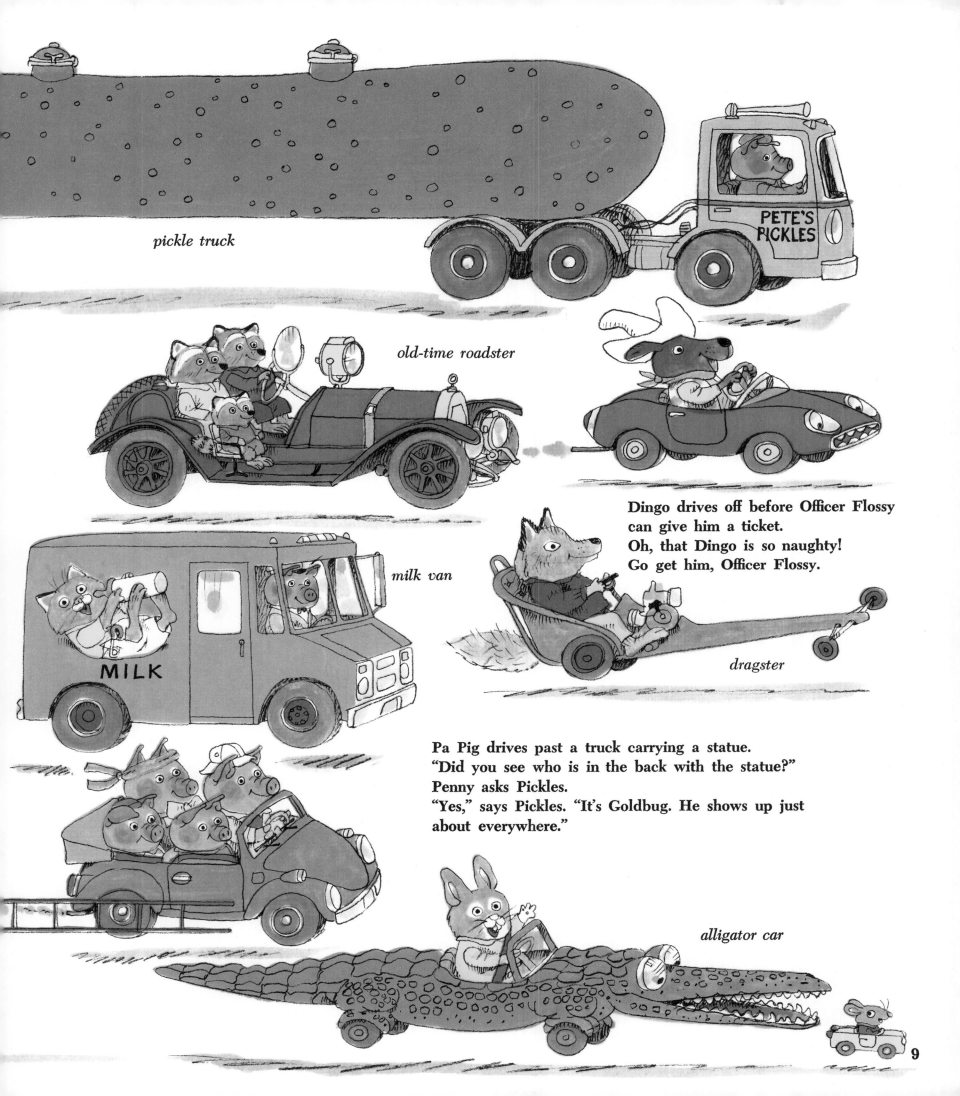

pickle truck

old-time roadster

milk van

Dingo drives off before Officer Flossy can give him a ticket. Oh, that Dingo is so naughty! Go get him, Officer Flossy.

dragster

Pa Pig drives past a truck carrying a statue. "Did you see who is in the back with the statue?" Penny asks Pickles. "Yes," says Pickles. "It's Goldbug. He shows up just about everywhere."

alligator car

steam locomotive

caboose

trailer

MOLASSES

tank truck

tilt-cab truck

10

Where is Goldbug now?
Is he riding in the locomotive?
Is he riding in the old-time buggy?
Can you find him?

old-time buggy

go-cart

tractor

three-wheel beet truck

canvas-cab truck

dumper

unicycle

sports car

MISTRESS MOUSE REPAIRS

The Pig family drives by a broken-down truck.
"It won't be broken down for long," says Pa. "I saw
Mistress Mouse working on it. She can fix almost anything."

11

workers' rest rooms

log loader

log skidder

The Pigs drive past a lumber camp.
The lumberjacks are busy gathering logs from the trees they have cut down.
The log-loader truck will take the logs to the sawmill.
There they will be cut into boards of all sizes, so houses and toys and all kinds of wooden things can be made from them.

crane

flat-bed trailer

12

forklift truck

log-loader truck

"Oh, Bunny Rabbit, look out," calls Penny Pig. "Don't get caught by that crane!"
Step on the gas, Bunny Rabbit!

13

Faster, Flossy, faster!
Go get Dingo!
But where is that rascal?
Can you see him?

JAKE THE PLUMBER

double cab pick-up

mouse van

pumpkin car

tractor

mobile crane

Homer drove his tractor into the pond.
That wasn't very smart, Homer.

bus

woody station wagon

Look! There is Mistress Mouse again. And this time she is towing a TOW TRUCK!
Hi there, Goldbug . . . wherever you are!

pig van

a wrecked car being towed
by a BIG TOW TRUCK which is being towed by a little tow truck

15

tourist bus

The baggage compartment on the bus has come open.
Someone's things are flying out!
Duck, Pa! Duck, Ma!
Oh dear, Ma didn't duck soon enough.

old-time fire engine

school mini-bus

dragster

MOTHER GOOSE
NURSERY SCHOOL

cheese truck

grain tank truck

ambulance

broom-o-cycle

sports car

My, there is a lot of traffic on the road today.
Firefighters are going to a fire.
Children are going to school.
A witch is going for a broom ride.
Go, everyone, go!

chopper bike

canvas-top car

big ditch-digger

Just look at all these machines!

**Some dig ditches.
Some lay water pipes.**

excavator

tiny ditch-digger

STOP

5-seater pencil car

auto transporter

street washer

18

pipelayer

tractor pipelayer

When the workers have finished, water will flow through these pipes into people's homes.

bulldozer

waterpipe carrier

road sweeper

Right now, water is flowing into the Pig family's car. I think someone had better fix that nozzle, don't you?

Goldbug car

rock dump truck

coal dump truck

My word! What is happening here?

Mrs. Rabbit calls to Mr. Rabbit to tell him where she wants him to dump the wheelbarrow. But Mr. Rabbit can't hear her.

So Mrs. Rabbit shouts as loud as she can, so loud that all the truckdrivers think she is shouting at them.

Goldbug dump truck

orange dump truck

wheelbarrow

toy dump truck

cement dump truck

tomato dump truck

sand side-dump truck

"DUMP IT THERE!" she shouts . . . and all the drivers dump their loads right THERE!

21

double-decker bus

FUEL OIL

fuel oil tank truck

refrigerator van

ICE CREAM

Land-Rover

old-time coupe

another 5-seater pencil car

22

trailer truck

old-time
double-decker bus

BOOKS ARE
FUN TO READ

READ ONE TODAY

2-seater crayon car

TV
REPAIR

TV repair car

light bulb
pick-up truck

Well, the orange-truck driver has given Penny and Pickles
an orange.
"I'm glad it wasn't the coal truck that dumped on us,"
says Pickles.

hitchhiker

jeep

"Look there!" says Penny. "I wonder if anyone would have
enough room to pick up that hitchhiker."
I think he had better start walking, don't you?

23

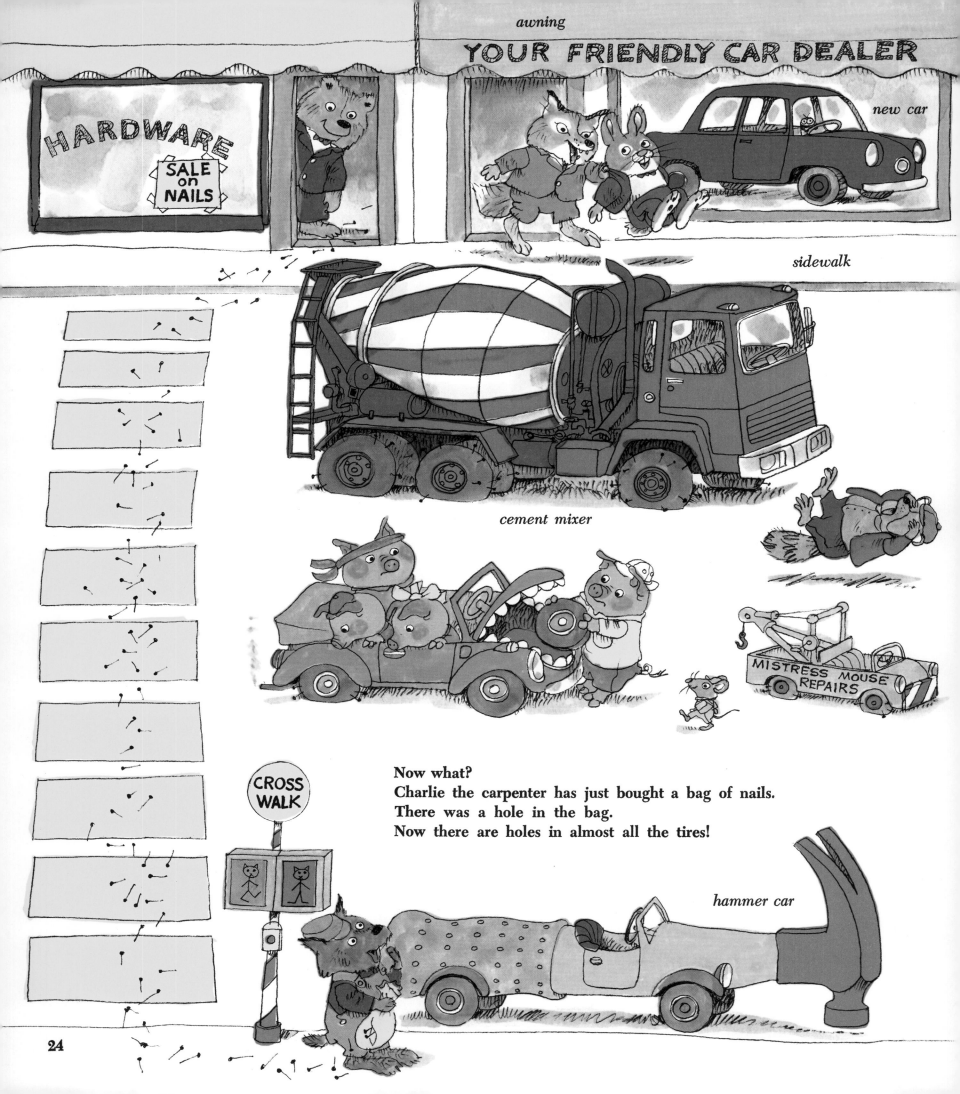

awning

YOUR FRIENDLY CAR DEALER

HARDWARE

SALE on NAILS

new car

sidewalk

cement mixer

MISTRESS MOUSE REPAIRS

CROSS WALK

Now what?
Charlie the carpenter has just bought a bag of nails.
There was a hole in the bag.
Now there are holes in almost all the tires!

hammer car

USED CARS

used car

school bus

SCHOOL BUS

hard hat

flat tire

antique buggy

cherry picker

Where's Dingo? How did he manage to get by without a flat tire? I see Officer Flossy is riding on the sidewalk.
Keep after him, Flossy!
Hi, Goldbug . . . wherever you are.

STOP

25

trolley bus

bug bus

motor scooter

SIGHTSEEING TOURS

sightseeing bus

yellow   violet

orange

brown

red

PAUL THE PAINTER

blue

green

pink

a painter's pick-up truck

sewer cleaner

ditch-digger

mobile crane

SQUEEZE LEFT
ROAD CONSTRUCTION
AHEAD

ant bus

hot dog car

rumble-seat roadster

coupe with open back hatch

Pa is all worn out from changing the
tire. He is taking a nap in the backseat
while Ma drives.
All right, everyone! Slow down! There is road
construction ahead.

coupe with open sunroof

dump truck

wheel loader

Goldbugdozer

dumped-over dump truck

motor grader

SPEED LIMIT
15
MPH

The heavy roadwork machines scrape and push the dirt and rocks about, to make a smooth roadbed for a new road.

four antique sports cars
Count them!

28

tractor scraper

dump truck

bulldozer

Pa wakes up from his nap.
He says to Penny, "I think the next car we buy will
be a bananamobile."
"Oh, goody," says Penny.
Would *you* like to have a bananamobile?

bananamobile

29

dumper trailer

off-highway tractor

Mistress Mouse pumping up a flat tire

tractor loader

MISTRESS MOUSE REPAIRS

Why don't you watch what you're doing?

auto-digger

Here are more workers and more roadwork machines. Some workers are not watching what their machines are doing!

dump truck

wheeled bulldozer

crawler tractor
ripping the ground

hippoloader

mouse ditch-digger

pickle car

Doctor Dentist's car

old-time car

Goldbug says to himself, "I must remember to make
an appointment with my dentist."
Where *is* Goldbug?

31

power shovel

rock crusher

motor grader

tamper-downer

limousine

teeny-tiny
limousine

mini-limousine

sports car

32

gravel dump truck

asphalt mixer

sand pile

dumper

crane

oil barrels

bucket loader

The roadbed is almost ready to be surfaced.
The rock crusher crushes big rocks into small stones.
Oil and sand are mixed together in the asphalt mixer and
out comes asphalt—hot, steaming asphalt.

taxi

carrotcar

"I think I would rather have
a carrotcar," says Pickles.

David Dog's car

33

gravel truck

asphalt oil spreader

stone spreader

custom buggy

Look out! Rollo Rabbit's steamroller has run away. Crunch! *CRUNCH!* CRUNCH! It has squashed three cars flat.

Look out, Flossy!
Look out, Mousie!
Look out, Ma!
Don't get squashed, too!

a runaway steamroller

STOP

guard rail

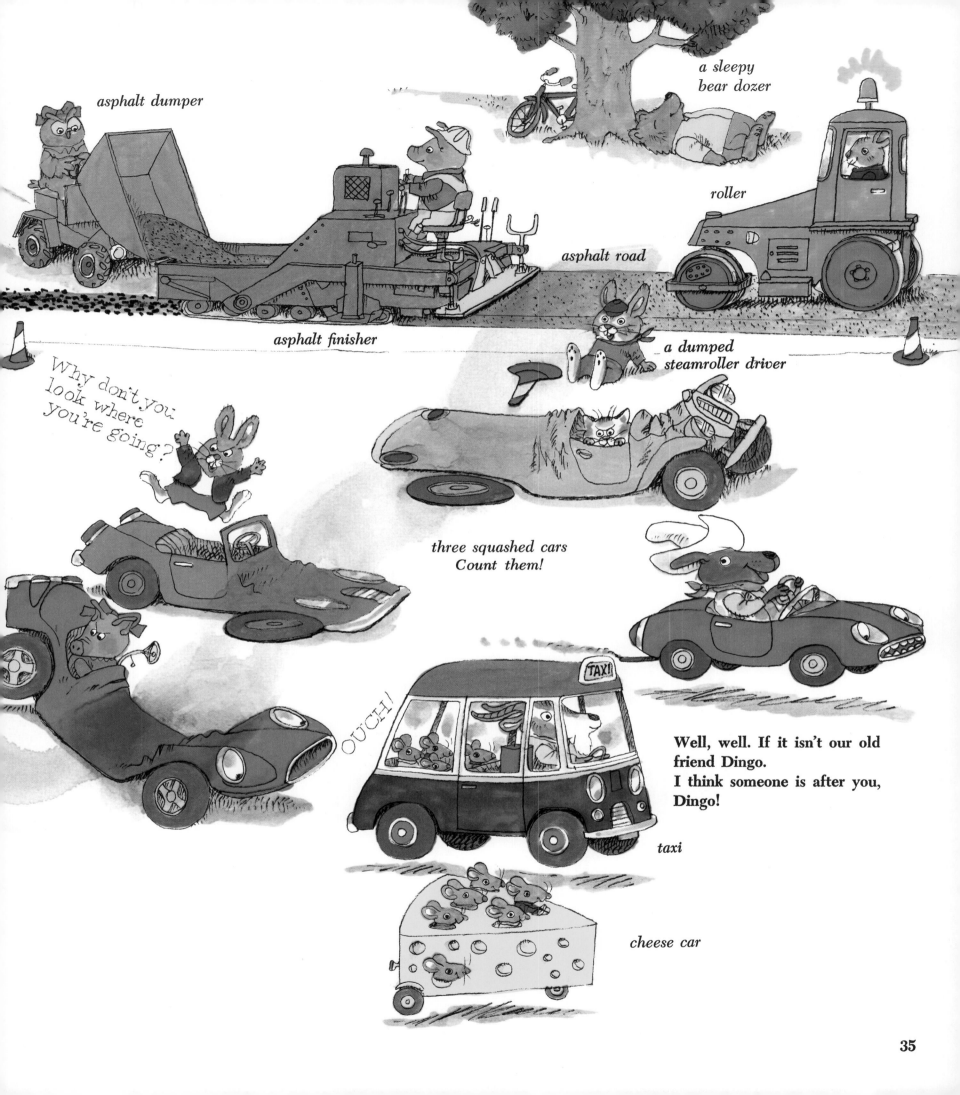

asphalt dumper

a sleepy bear dozer

roller

asphalt road

asphalt finisher

a dumped steamroller driver

Why don't you look where you're going?

three squashed cars
Count them!

OUCH!

Well, well. If it isn't our old friend Dingo.
I think someone is after you, Dingo!

taxi

cheese car

35

roller

The workers are finishing the new road.
The last thing they have to do is paint the dividing lines.

highway stripers

KEEP LEFT

camper

FRESH EGGS

egg truck

airport limousine

AIRPORT LIMOUSINE

motorcycle

motor scooter

2-seater bicycle

Maniacbug

Say! Who is that making a mess of the line? That's not Goldbug, is it?
No, it can't be Goldbug. He would never do a thing like that. That fellow must be Maniacbug.

sports roadster

bookshelf maker's car

Keep left, everyone. Drive slowly onto the new road.

farm tractor

a tired traveler

hay-and-pig wagon (Make a wish!)

mini-bus

antique car

STOP

GAS →

toothbrush car

gasoline tank truck

GASOLINE

gas pump

hose

car washer

REST ROOMS

a woodchuck
in a hurry

CAR WASH

mini-jeep

old-time buggy

toothpaste car

EXIT

oil cans

attendant

Ma Pig sees that they are running low on gas, so she drives into the gas station to fill up the tank. I can find Goldbug, but I can't see the Pig family. Where do you suppose they have gone?

dirty station wagon

auto lift

car greaser

hook-and-ladder truck

7

rescue truck

ALL RIGHT!
Who left the water
running in that
fire engine?

4

1

water tower truck

fire alarm box

siren

40

hose

Fire Chief's car

CHIEF

The Pig family is all refreshed. The gas tank is full again, and Pa is back at the wheel.

nozzle

ambulance

Ladybug has a fire in her car and the fire fighters have come to put it out.
Can you guess who called them?

helmet

bell

pumper truck

fire hydrant

diesel locomotive

mail car

tank car

boxcar

forklift

All the wheels need to be oiled so they won't squeak. Squeaky Mouse says so.

antique car

Tom Turtle's car

gardener's truck

42

auto carrier car

double-decker coach car

steam locomotive

railroad station

CLOVER

station wagon

doughnut car

Railroad stations are busy places. There are always lots of people coming and going. Freight trains load and unload letters, food, packages, and all sorts of things.

Some people like to go far away for their vacation. If they want to have their car to drive, they can take it along on the train's auto carrier car.

"I hope I remembered to put doughnuts in the picnic basket," Ma says to herself.
I wonder what made her think of that?

racing cars

bigshot car

canvas-roof car

old-time racing car

pick-up truck

"Look," says Penny, "an auto race!"
"I'm too hungry to look," says Pickles.
"Now just be patient," says Ma. "It won't be long before we have our picnic. But first we must stop at Grandma Pig's farm and buy some fresh corn."

MR. GREEN THUMB GARDENER

VAROOM! VAROOM!
VAROOM!
And the winner is . . .
MISTRESS MOUSE!

mouse-car transporter

COME TO THE
CIRCUS
NOW PLAYING

rhinoceros car

sunroof car

45

corn picker

hay gatherer

At Grandma Pig's farm, all the farmhands are very busy.
They are picking corn, gathering hay, and delivering milk.
They are harvesting wheat to be made into bread.
Grandpa is cutting the grass and Grandma is clanking
around on her old steam tractor.
My! What a busy farm!

milk cans

corn car

Auntie Pastry and Cousin Willie are selling fresh corn.
It looks so good, Pa just has to take a bite.
"No, Pa," says Ma. "Don't eat it yet! Wait until I cook it!"

well

FRESH
CORN

grain harvester

wheat

tractor

Grandma's steam tractor

grass cutter

Wolfwagon

47

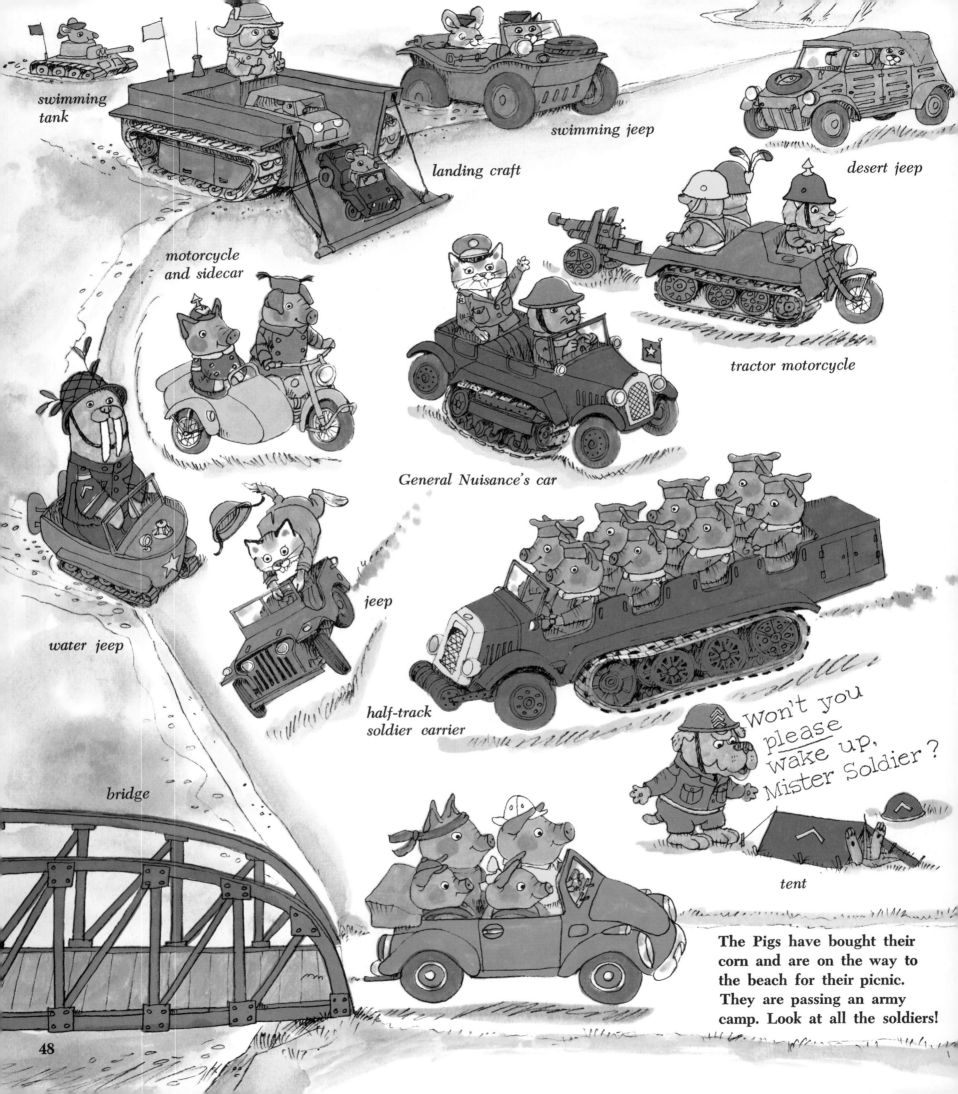

swimming
tank

swimming jeep

landing craft

desert jeep

motorcycle
and sidecar

tractor motorcycle

General Nuisance's car

water jeep

jeep

half-track
soldier carrier

Won't you
please
wake up,
Mister Soldier?

bridge

tent

The Pigs have bought their
corn and are on the way to
the beach for their picnic.
They are passing an army
camp. Look at all the soldiers!

48

chapel truck

canteen truck

radio truck

old-time tank

ambulance

antique armored car

tank

army car

gun tractor

These soldiers are going home for the weekend to visit their families. Their car is just like an army car, but it is painted differently.

civilian car

tail

a worker washing a jet plane

Hey! Watch it!

mouse monoplane

cherry picker

wing

SWISSAIR

stewardess

ladder

jet engine

jet-fuel truck

food truck

baggage train

spilled baggage

50

mouse
pusher-plane

mouse triplane

Hey, Pa! What are you doing driving through the airport? That sign saying "Follow me" does not mean *you*! That follow-me car shows airplanes where to park after they land.

Look! That crazy Dingo is following it, too! I wonder — is Officer Flossy still following Dingo?

Hey! Watch it!

mouse biplane

pilot

follow-me car

nose

airmail truck

AIR MAIL

FOLLOW ME

generator truck

tractor

MISTRESS MOUSE REPAIRS

a crash landing

mobile apartment house

sun-roof camper

mobile home

Kitty camper

roof-bed camper

grill with two burned hot dogs

"I do hope we get to the beach soon," says Pa.

52

trailer home

old-school-bus home

swimming-pool truck

just-a-little-bit-too-small camper

The Hogs are spending their vacation at a trailer camp. "We don't seem to be able to get through the gate," Mama Hog says to Papa Hog. "I wonder if we should leave a few things at home next year?"

HAPPY HOURS CAMP

HOG HEAVEN

PLEASE WIPE FEET

NO RIDERS

There's Officer Flossy! Go get him, Flossy!

53

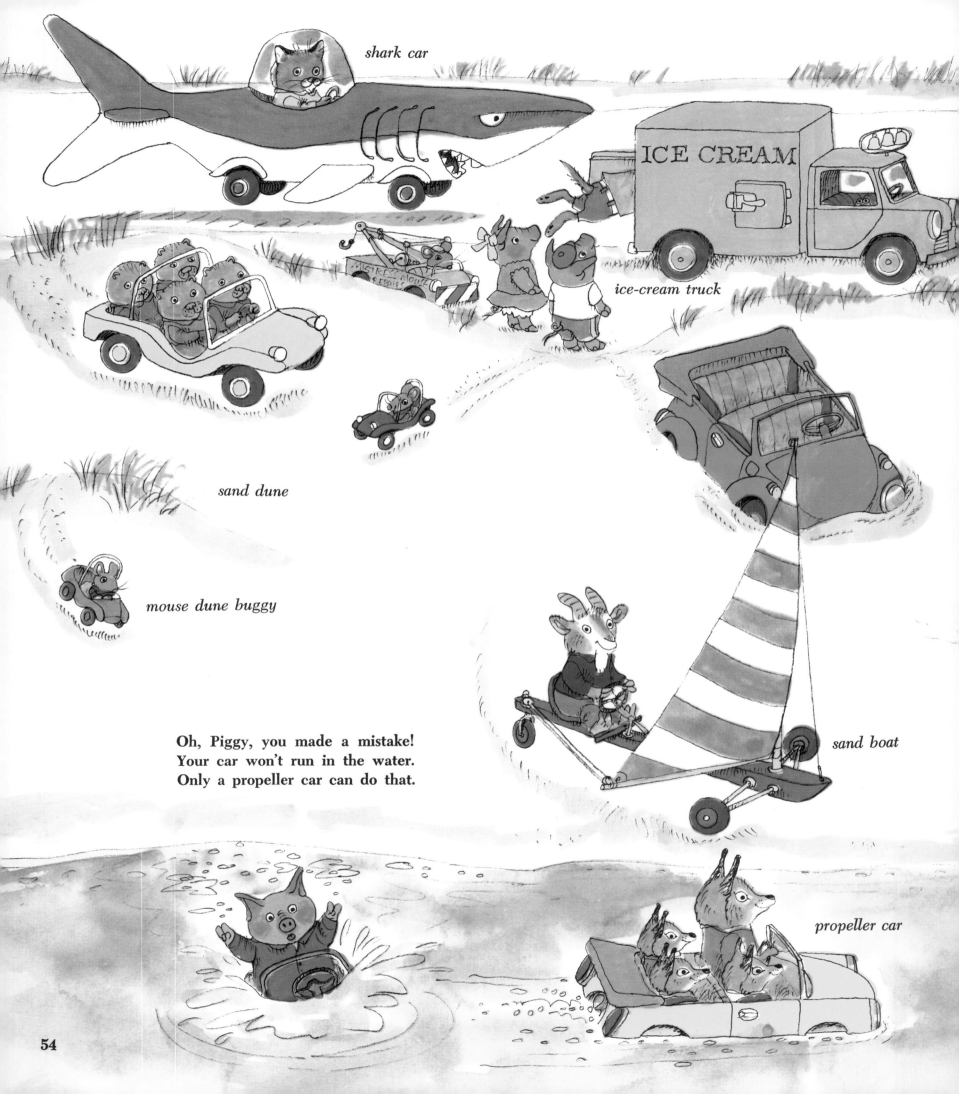

shark car

ICE CREAM

ice-cream truck

sand dune

mouse dune buggy

sand boat

Oh, Piggy, you made a mistake!
Your car won't run in the water.
Only a propeller car can do that.

propeller car

surrey car

BATH HOUSE

shower

refreshment stand

dune buggies

Roll bars protect
the driver in case
the buggy rolls over.

"AT LAST!" says Ma. "We are at the
beach and we are going to have a nice
quiet picnic. Pa, maybe you should put
a shirt on. I think you are getting
sunburned."
"Oh, I'll be all right," says Pa.

go-anywhere buggy

pedal boat

submarine

55

forklift

The picnic is over, and Pa is not all right.
He is all RED! WOW! What a sunburn!
Pa is also all stuffed, with food. A nap is
just what he needs, so Ma drives for a while.
Close your mouth when you sleep, Pa!

dock

propeller

tugboat

air-cushion ferry (hovercraft)

FERRY

TICKET
OFFICE

FERRY

crane

radar

flag

smokestack

lifeboat

anchor

a furious captain

cargo freighter

a falling car

tender car

barge

Pa is missing all the sights of the harbor. Cars are being loaded onto a freighter, to be carried across the ocean to far parts of the world.

Oh, my! One of them is not going any farther than the bottom of the harbor!

straddle truck

flying fish

FISH

fish truck

57

garbage truck

WATCH WHAT YOU'RE DOING!!

squasher-downer

bulldozer

a squashed-down golf cart

Two golfers have lost their golf balls in the garbage dump. Please help find them.

TOWN DUMP

caterpillar bus

cross-country car

58

The Pig family is driving up into the mountains. It is getting colder. It is snowing. The road is icy. The pie truck skids off the road.
Mistress Mouse says it is time to put on snow chains. Hey Pa! Wake up! Put on your snow chains! And please put the top up.

a skidding pie truck

MOM'S PIES

icy road

SLIPPERY WHEN WET

bent sign

MISTRESS MOUSE REPAIRS

a worker stringing wire on telephone poles

TELEPHONE COMPANY

spool of wire

telephone truck

snow bus

Ma put on the snow chains.
Ma put the top up.
WOW! Just look at all that snow! Isn't it beautiful?
There's a pile of things all covered with snow on the truck
behind the Pigs. I wonder what they could be?

Harry, dear!
You must remember
to close the
window
after you!

snowplow

60

sled

Backwoodsman Bear taking home some honey on his snowmobile

HONEY

snow tractor pulling a roller to pack the snow down on the ski slope for better skiing

roller

skier

a mouse packing down snow

snow blower

guide poles for snowplowing

61

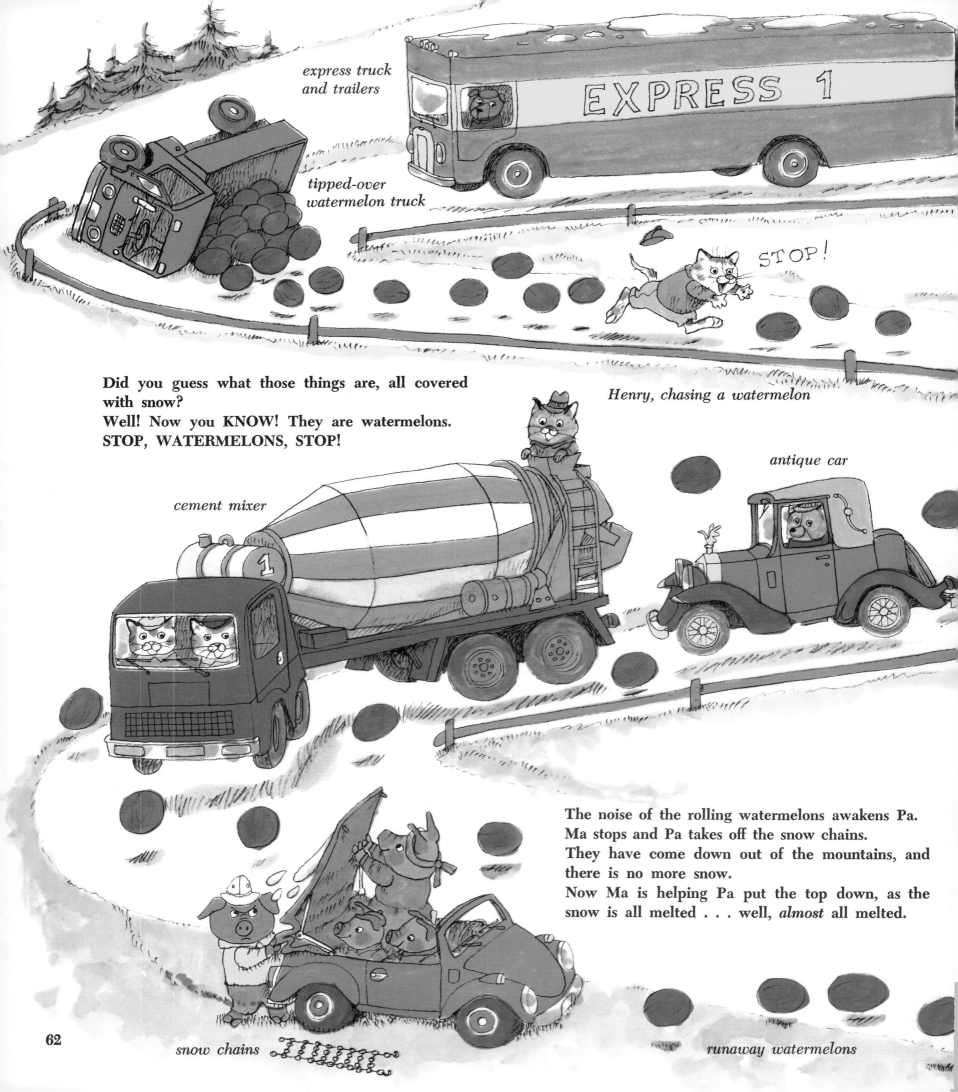

express truck
and trailers

EXPRESS 1

tipped-over
watermelon truck

STOP!

Did you guess what those things are, all covered
with snow?
Well! Now you KNOW! They are watermelons.
STOP, WATERMELONS, STOP!

Henry, chasing a watermelon

antique car

cement mixer

The noise of the rolling watermelons awakens Pa.
Ma stops and Pa takes off the snow chains.
They have come down out of the mountains, and
there is no more snow.
Now Ma is helping Pa put the top down, as the
snow is all melted . . . well, *almost* all melted.

snow chains

runaway watermelons

EXPRESS 2

EXPRESS 3

chemical
tank truck

mountain
climber

Harry, chasing
a watermelon

STOP!

Carl Cat's car

roadster

skis on a rack

snowshoe

SKI SCHOOL

ski-school bus

63

Oh, NO!
I never thought I would see an accident as bad as this one! This is what I would call SOME ACCIDENT!
It just doesn't seem possible, does it?
But there you are . . . you can see for yourself.
And poor Mistress Mouse! It will probably take her a MILLION YEARS to fix everything.
Luckily, no one was badly hurt.

WHIPPED CREAM

FIRE DE

FLOUR

TOMATO JUICE

BANANAS

FRESH EGGS

MISTRESS MOUSE REPAIRS

The egg men always wear seat belts so that they won't fall out and get broken. Do you?

"Well, we are almost home now," says Pa.
"Thank goodness," says Ma.

65

And, sure enough, here they are.
"BACK, SAFE, HOME AGAIN," they all say together.
In front of their house, a delivery man is just leaving.
"What are those boxes on the front lawn?" asks Ma.
"What are those boxes on the front lawn?" asks Penny.
"What are those boxes on the front lawn?" asks Pickles.
Pa just smiles and doesn't ask anything.
"Oh, look!" says Ma. "I think we are going to have new neighbors."

delivery van

advertising car

mobile library

66

68

And, sure enough, Ma is right, as usual. They *do* have new neighbors.
And Penny and Pickles—and Goldbug, too!—have new automobiles!
Pa bought them at the toy shop at the start of their trip.
Do you remember his visit to the toy shop?

Hi!

Hi!

Hi!

Hi!

Hi!

Hi!

Hi!

Hi!

Hi!

Hi!

Hi!

Hi!

Hi!

Hi!

Hi!

Hi!

Hi!

Hi!

Hi!

Hi!

F.D

POLICE

7

Well, at last! Officer Flossy has finally caught that Dingo. When will he ever learn to drive properly? Probably never . . . but we can always hope for the best. My! Hasn't it been an exciting day?

Yikes!

STOP

THIS IS THE END